Chuck E. was a very healthy young beaver. He didn't have to go to Dr. Woodchuck's office very often. Many times over the last year Chuck E. had gone with his mother and father to the doctor's office so that his baby sister Bonnie could get her vaccinations and checkups. Chuck E. was relieved to think that his own vaccinations and checkups were all done with. But kids need to go for checkups every year, and sometimes they need booster shots too.

THE ADVENTURES OF "CHUCK E. BEAVER" AND FRIENDS

THE VISIT TO DR. WOODCHUCK

Written by
KiKi

Illustrated by
GEORGE ELLIOTT

Published by
Montbec Inc.

Publisher
MATT ARENY

Publication Advisor
JOSE AZEVEDO

Editorial Supervisor
ETHEL SALTZMAN

Artwork Supervisor
PIERRE RENAUD

ISBN 2-89227-222-X

Near the end of the week, Mr. and Mrs. Beaver had made an appointment to bring Bonnie in to see Dr. Woodchuck for a checkup and for her fourteen month's vaccination. Her appointment was for four o'clock on Friday, and they decided that it would be best if Chuck E. went with them after school.

At dinner time on Thursday, Mrs. Beaver received a phone call from Dr. Woodchuck's office.

"Hello, Mrs. Beaver?" Dr. Woodchuck
asked, when Mrs. Beaver picked up the
phone. "This is Dr. Woodchuck calling.
I just wanted to remind you of Bonnie's
appointment for tomorrow, and to tell
you that Chuck E. is due for a checkup
and his vaccination as well," the doctor
said.

"Oh, is it time for his booster already?" Mrs. Beaver asked.

"Yes, it is, and I thought it would be convenient for you all if he could see me tomorrow too," Dr. Woodchuck said.

"Well, Chuck E.'s coming with us, so that will be just fine," Mrs. Beaver agreed. "I'll let him know."

While Mrs. Beaver was on the phone with Dr. Woodchuck, Chuck E. couldn't help overhearing their conversation. When she came back into the dining room, Chuck E. asked her what the phone call was all about.

"That was Dr. Woodchuck, Chuck E.," Mrs. Beaver replied. "He called about Bonnie's appointment tomorrow and to tell me that you're also due for a checkup and a booster."

"But I'm not sick, Mom," Chuck E. pleaded. "So why do I have to go to the doctor's office?"

"It's important to have a checkup at least once a year so that we make sure you're growing well,"
Mrs. Beaver explained. "The booster shot, as you know from watching your baby sister, is to protect you from getting a serious illness. You understand why it's necessary, don't you?"

"I guess so, but I don't like going to see Dr. Woodchuck because I feel embarrassed about taking my clothes off," Chuck E. said nervously. "It's not like I'm afraid of needles or anything, but I'd feel a lot better if you or Dad came in with me."

"Sure, son, we'd be happy to!" Mr. Beaver reassured him. "We understand how you feel. Even your mother and I still feel a bit uncomfortable when we have to go to the doctor's office. So you see you're not alone."

"Really, Mom?" Chuck E. asked.

"Yes, son," Mrs. Beaver confirmed. "I don't like going to the doctor's office any more than you do, but I know it's for my own good! Sometimes we have to do things we don't really like, but we can feel good that we're taking care of ourselves, right, son?"

"You're right, Mom," Chuck E. agreed. "And that's what I'm going to do."

The next day, Chuck E. went with his parents and Bonnie to Dr. Woodchuck's office. As they entered the reception area, Chuck E. noticed Wally Wolverine, sitting with his parents and looking extremely nervous. Chuck E. went over to see Wally, while Mr. and Mrs. Beaver checked in with Dr. Woodchuck's receptionist.

"Hi, Wally! Are you here to see Dr. Woodchuck, too?" Chuck E. asked curiously.

"Uh-Uh, yeah," Wally replied nervously as he stared blankly into the air. "Why are you here?"

"Oh, I'm here for a checkup and my booster shot," Chuck E. said rather nonchalantly. "Why are you here?"

"S-S-Same thing," Wally remarked, looking frightened. "Aren't you scared of getting your shot?" he asked.

"Oh, a bit," Chuck E. answered truthfully, "but my father convinced me that being afraid is nothing to be ashamed of. If you want to know something, my father still gets nervous about seeing Dr. Woodchuck." Chuck E. was trying to help Wally feel better.

"R-R-Really?" Wally remarked with surprise. "I guess if it's okay for him to be afraid, then it's okay for me to be afraid too."

"Sure!" Chuck E. said. "Say, why don't we do this together?"

"Do you think your parents would let us?" Wally asked hopefully.

"I don't see why not!" Chuck E. answered. "I'll ask them. I'm sure if it's okay with Dr. Woodchuck, then it'll be okay with them."

"Gee, that would be great!" Wally said excitedly.

Chuck E. went back to where his parents were sitting, and asked whether he and Wally could get their shots together.

"I don't see why not," Mrs. Beaver replied. "We'll ask Dr. Woodchuck."

Soon Dr. Woodchuck came out of his office and called for Mr. and Mrs. Wolverine to bring Wally in for his examination. Before they took Wally into the examination room, Mrs. Beaver and Chuck E. went up to talk to Dr. Woodchuck.

"Oh, hello Mrs. Beaver, Chuck E.," Dr. Woodchuck said politely. "How are you today?" he asked.

"We're just fine, doctor," Mrs. Beaver responded. "We wanted to ask you if it would be alright if Chuck E. and his friend Wally could get their shots together."

"Why, sure!" Dr. Woodchuck exclaimed with a smile. "That's a terrific idea, Chuck E! I'll give you your examinations first, and then you can both come in and get your shots together, okay?"

"Great!" Chuck E. replied, as he smiled over at Wally.

Dr. Woodchuck examined Wally first, then Chuck E. He looked at their throats, eyes, and ears. He checked their weight and height. He listened to their chests with a stethoscope and poked around their tummies to see if everything was okay on the inside. He took their temperatures, which were normal, and completed their examinations with an eye test. Everything checked out fine. Now it was time for their booster shots.

Dr. Woodchuck asked Wally and Chuck E. to come into another room.

"You can bring your parents if you like," he suggested.

"No, we'll do this ourselves!" Chuck E. said proudly. "Right, Wally?"

"R-Right, Chuck E!" Wally stammered. Dr. Woodchuck got the needles ready for their shots.

"So who would like to go first?" the
doctor asked, holding a needle in the air.

"W-W-Why don't you go first, Chuck
E?" Wally suggested, as he stepped back
from Dr. Woodchuck in fear.

36

"Gee, I-I don't know," Chuck E. said.
"Is this going to hurt?"

"No, son, you won't feel a thing.
I promise!" Dr. Woodchuck replied,
trying to calm Chuck E.

"Okay, but remember you promised,"
Chuck E. agreed, and he rolled up his
sleeve.

Dr. Woodchuck had Chuck E. sit up on the examination table and gave him his shot very quickly. Chuck E. kept his eyes closed very tightly, and gritted his teeth the whole time in preparation for the needle. When it was all over, Chuck E. was still gritting his teeth with his eyes closed.

"You can open your eyes now, Chuck E. It's all over!" Dr. Woodchuck stated.

"It is?" Chuck E. asked in amazement. "But I didn't feel anything!"

"I told you you wouldn't feel anything," Dr. Woodchuck explained.

"You were right!" Chuck E. agreed, rolling his sleeve back down. "Wally, there's nothing to be afraid of!"

"Okay, if you say so," Wally replied, looking a little less nervous. He jumped up on the table, and he too received his shot without any pain.

Wally and Chuck E. got dressed and went back to the reception area where their parents were waiting.

"So, son, how was it?" Mr. Beaver asked.

"Didn't feel a thing, Pop!" Chuck E. said proudly. "Isn't that right, Wally?" he asked, looking over at Wally with a smile.

"That's right, Chuck E!" Wally agreed enthusiastically. "Those needles don't scare us!" he boasted.

"Well, we're proud of both of you!"
Mrs. Beaver said. "You're two brave
boys!"

After that day, Chuck E. and Wally
returned to see Dr. Woodchuck every
year for their checkups. They were a bit
nervous every time they came in, but they
were never really afraid again.

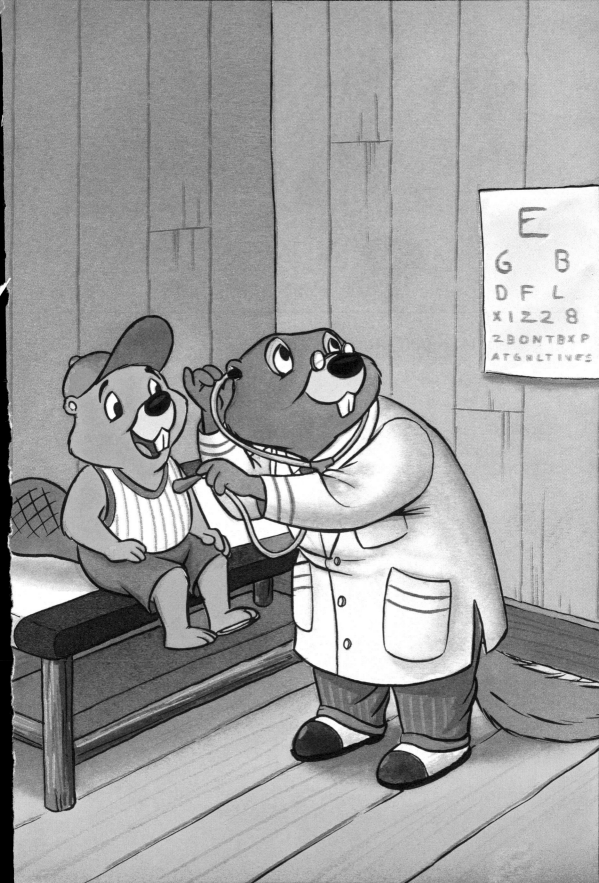

Seeing the doctor once a year

Is important for everyone!

It helps to keep us from getting sick,

And we all know that's no fun.

Your friend,

Chuck E.